The Funny Zone

ANIMAL ZONE

Read Jokes. Write Jokes.

Jokes, Riddles, Tongue Twisters & "Daffynitions"

By Gary Chmielewski

Illustrated by Jim Caputo

A Note to Parents and Caregivers:

As the old saying goes, "Laughter is the best medicine." It's true for reading as well. Kids naturally love humor, so why not look to their interests to get them motivated to read? The Funny Zone series features books that include jokes, riddles, word plays, and tongue twisters-all of which are sure to delight your young reader.

We invite you to share this book with your child, taking turns to read aloud to one another, practicing timing, emphasis, and expression. You and your child can deliver the jokes in a natural voice, or have fun creating character voices and exaggerating funny words. Be sure to pause often to make sure your child understands the jokes. Talk about what you are reading and use this opportunity to explore new vocabulary words and ideas. Reading aloud can help your child build confidence in reading.

Along with being fun and motivating, humorous text involves higher order thinking skills that support comprehension. Jokes, riddles, and word plays require us to explore the creative use of language, develop word and sound recognition, and expand vocabulary.

At the end of the book there are activities to help your child develop writing skills. These activities tap your child's creativity by exploring numerous types of humor. Children who write materials based on the activities are encouraged to send them to Norwood House Press for publication on our website or in future books. Please see page 24 for details.

Above all, the most important part of the reading experience is to have fun and enjoy it!

Sincerely,

Shannon Cannon

Shannon Cannon
Literacy Consultant

NORWOOD HOUSE PRESS

P.O. Box 316598 • Chicago, Illinois 60631
For information regarding Norwood House Press, please visit our website at:
www.norwoodhousepress.com or call 866-565-2900.

Designer: Design Lab
Project Management: Editorial Directions

Library of Congress Cataloging-in-Publication Data:
Chmielewski, Gary, 1946–
  The animal zone / by Gary Chmielewski ; illustrated by Jim Caputo.
    p. cm. — (The funny zone)
Summary: "Contains animal-themed jokes for children as well as exercises
to teach children how to write their own jokes"—Provided by publisher.
  ISBN-13: 978-1-59953-139-7 (library edition : alk. paper)
  ISBN-10: 1-59953-139-9 (library edition : alk. paper)
  1. Animals—Juvenile humor. I. Caputo, Jim. II. Title.
  PN6231.A5C48 2008
  818'.5402—dc22   2007007503

Printed in the United States of America

AT HOME

Teacher: "If there are ten cats in a boat and one jumps out, how many are left?"
Jeffrey: "None, they all were copycats!"

"It's raining cats and dogs today."
"I know. I just stepped into a poodle."

A farmer riding a horse saw a dog on the road.

"Good morning," said the dog.

"I didn't know dogs could talk," said the farmer out loud.

"Neither did I," said the horse.

MOUSETRAP
A cat

Which dog always knows what time it is?

A watch dog!

SOURPUSS
A cat who eats lemons

When is it proper to serve milk in a saucer?

When you feed a cat!

PUT OUT
How the cat feels at night

Laura was walking her dog. A policeman came by and asked,

"Does that dog have a license?"

"He doesn't need one," replied Laura. "He isn't old enough to drive!"

4

Maria: "I've got a cat who can say his own name."

Emily: "That's great. What's your cat's name?"

Maria: "Meow!"

If a dog chews shoes, what shoes should he choose to chew?

What kind of dog does a person bite?

A hot dog!

What's the opposite of a cool cat?

A hot dog!

DACHSHUND

A real down-to-earth dog

James: "I can yell 'Spot, Spot, Spot' all day and my dog won't come to me."

Darrell: "Why not?"

James: "His name is Fred!"

What kind of dog hands out tickets?

A police dog!

What kind of cat hangs around a bowling alley?

An alley cat!

Why does a dog wag its tail?

Because no one else will wag it for him!

What is a good way to keep a dog off the street?

Put him in a barking lot!

Veterinarian: "Has your dog ever had fleas?"

Susan: "No, only puppies!"

Chris: "My cat Maddie is sick, so we're taking her to the animal doctor."

Alan: "Gee, I thought all doctors were people."

What's a fighter's favorite dog?

A boxer!

David: "We have a new dog."

Gail: "What's he like?"

David: "Anything we feed him!"

What do dogs and trees have in common?

Their bark!

James: "Your dog just bit my ankle."

Lisa: "What did you expect? He's just a small dog and can't reach any higher!"

Lupita: "How much are those kittens in the window?"

Pet Store Owner: "Thirty dollars apiece."

Lupita: "How much is a whole one?"

What kind of dog can be found at the bowling alley?

A setter!

Kevin: "My parents bought me a bird for my birthday."

Jade: "What kind?"

Kevin: "A keet."

Jade: "Don't you mean a parakeet?"

Kevin: "No, they only bought me one!"

AT THE ZOO

Mother tiger to baby tiger: "What are you doing?"

Baby tiger: "I'm chasing a hunter around the tree."

Mother tiger: "How often do I have to tell you not to play with your food!"

ZOOKEEPER

A critter sitter

Why was the baby raised on monkey milk?

Because it was a baby monkey!

How do you know an elephant will stay for a long time when it comes to visit?

It brings its trunk!

CAMELOT
A place where they sell used camels

Why did the elephant quit the circus?
He didn't want to work for peanuts anymore!

Why does the elephant wear dark glasses?

If you had all those jokes told about you, wouldn't you hide too?

How do you get down from an elephant?

You don't. You get down from a duck or goose!

What animal hides in a grape?

An ape!

What animal eats with its tail?

They all do. No animal removes its tail to eat.

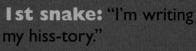

1st snake: "I'm writing my hiss-tory."

2nd snake: "I'm a writer too. I write boa-graphies!"

What did the elephant say when she sat on the box of cookies?

"That's the way the cookies crumble!"

Silent snakes slipping slowly southwards.

UNDER WATER

Park Ranger: "Young man, there's no fishing here!"

Young Man: "You're telling me. I haven't caught anything in two hours!"

SANDBAR
A place where fish can get a soda

Little Girl: "What kind of fish is that?"

Fisherman: "Smelt."

Little Girl: "It sure does. But what kind of fish is it?"

What marine animal goes well with peanut butter in your sandwich?

A jellyfish!

I never smelled a smelt that smelled as bad as that smelt smelled.

SANDBANK
A place where fish keep their money

Tony: "I went swimming today and a fish bit one of my fingers."

Cori: "Which one?"

Tony: "I don't know. All fish look alike!"

What did one fish say to the other fish after it was hooked?

"That's what you get for not keeping your mouth shut!"

What are the smartest animals in the sea?

Fish — they go around in schools.

SNAP! SNAP!

Michael: "I've got an alligator on my boat named Ginger."

Sandy: "Does Ginger bite?"

Michael: "No, Ginger snaps!"

ON THE HUNT

Park Ranger: "Do you know you're hunting with last year's license?"

Charles: "It's okay. I'm only after the ones that got away last year!"

First Hunter: "I just ran into a big bear!"

Second Hunter: "Did you let him have both barrels?"

First Hunter: "Both barrels? I let him have the whole gun!"

First Hunter: "This must be a good place for hunting."

Second Hunter: "How do you know?"

First Hunter: "The sign said 'Fine For Hunting'."

ON THE FARM

What do you call a cow laying down?

Ground Beef!

BULLDOZER
A sleeping bull

A donkey seeing a zebra for the first time said to himself: "Imagine that! A donkey that's been to jail!"

WANTED

Ray: "Does your cow give milk?"

Kathryn: "No. We have to take it from her!"

Why shouldn't you cry when a cow falls on the ice?

It's no use crying over spilled milk!

16

Sheep shouldn't sleep
in a shack,
Sheep should sleep
in a shed.

**Does horseback
riding give you
a headache?**
No, quite the reverse!

Why was the chicken farmer at the basketball game?

He was looking for fowls!

**Why did the farmer
put bells on his cows?**
Their horns didn't work!

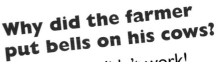

OUT OF ORDER

CLANG
CLANG

What is cow hide used for?

To hold the cow
together!

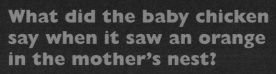

What did the baby chicken say when it saw an orange in the mother's nest?

"Look at the orange Mama laid!"

17

Why is it hard to talk with a goat around?

He always butts in!

She'll call you back.

That's my phone!

What should you do when a bull charges you?

Pay him!

Steven: "I went riding today."

Danita: "Horseback?"

Steven: "Sure – about two hours before me."

A young man was helping a farmer herd some cattle when the farmer asked him to hold the bull for a moment.

"No sir," said the young man. "I don't mind being a director in this operation, but I don't want to be a stockholder!"

IN THE BACKYARD

NUTCRACKER SUITE
A squirrel's home

Teacher: "Brent, use 'defeat', 'defense', and 'detail' in a sentence."

Brent: "The fox cut across the field, and defeat went over the defense before detail!"

Wriggly worms squirm regularly.

Knock, knock.

Who's there?

Gopher!

Gopher who?

Gopher a touchdown!

What does a skunk do when it's angry?

It raises a stink!

Why is a rabbit's nose always shiny?

Because its powder puff is on the wrong end!

Did you ever see a gopher go for a gopher hole?

Yes! I saw a gopher go for a gopher hole when I was going for the gopher.

19

IN THE SKY

HUMMINGBIRD
A bird that doesn't know the words

Put three ducks in a box. What do you get?
A box of quackers!

ILLEGAL
A big sick bird

What bird is at your meal?
A swallow!

What do you call a duck that steals from banks?
A safe quacker!

What has a pelican got in common with the Water Company?

They both have large bills!

What animals do you find at every baseball game?

Bats!

Tina: "Did you hear the story about the peacock?"

Janine: "No."

Tina: Well, it's a beautiful tale ..."

What's a boxer's favorite bird?

A duck!

Why do ducks dive?

They want to liquidate their bills!

BUGGING YOU

Why do bees hum?

They don't know
the words!

RELIGIOUS INSECT

Praying Mantis

**What do bees do
with their honey?**

They cell it!

Teacher: "William, how can
you prevent diseases caused by
biting insects?"

William: "Don't bite any!"

Why does a spider make a good baseball player?

Because it catches flies!

HORSEFLY
A fly with laryngitis

What did one firefly say to the other firefly?

"Your son sure is bright for his age!"

WRITING JOKES CAN BE AS MUCH FUN AS READING THEM!

Riddles are one of the most popular kinds of jokes. A riddle is usually a short question followed by a short answer. It might be a pun (a joke based on a word that has two meanings or two words that sound the same but have different meanings). It might also show a different way to look at a person, place, or thing. Here is a riddle from page 18:

What should you do when a bull charges you?

Pay him!

To understand this joke you have to know that "charge" can have different meanings: 1) *to rush at in order to attack* or 2) *to ask someone to pay a certain price for something*. It's funny because people think of the first definition of charging when they think of a bull, but the author of the joke uses the second definition instead.

Go back and re-read all the jokes in this book. Identify the jokes that are riddles. Which ones do you think are funny? Think about the different meanings of key words and how they are used to make a funny riddle.

YOU TRY IT!

You can do this joke-writing exercise with a group of friends or by yourself. Spend a few minutes picking an animal to write a riddle about (for example: cat, dog, alligator, whale, kangaroo, etc.) Next, everyone takes turns naming certain things about the animal: things they do, sounds they make, what they look like, etc. Don't stop to think about whether the words would be good for writing animal riddles, just list everything that comes to mind.

Once you have a list of words that describe the animal, use this list to help construct your riddle about the animal. Have everyone take turns coming up with a riddle using the words given. Write all the riddles down.

Whether you worked in a group or alone, test out your jokes on friends or family who haven't heard them yet. Did they laugh? If they did, that's a good sign that other people will like it too.

SEND US YOUR JOKES!

Pick out the best riddle that you created and send it to us at Norwood House Press. We will publish it on our website — organized according to grade level, the state you live in, and your first name.

Selected jokes might also appear in a future special edition book *Kids Write in the Funny Zone*. If your joke is included in the book, you and your school will receive a free copy.

Here's how to send the jokes to Norwood House Press:

1) Go to www.norwoodhousepress.com.
2) Click on the **Enter the Funny Zone** tab.
3) Select and print the joke submission form.
4) Fill out the form, include your joke, and send to:
   The Funny Zone
   Norwood House Press
   PO Box 316598
   Chicago, IL 60631

Here's how to see your joke posted on the website:

1) Go to www.norwoodhousepress.com.
2) Click on the **Enter the Funny Zone** tab.
3) Select **Kids Write in the Funny Zone** tab.
4) Locate your grade level, then state, then first name.
   If it's not there yet check back again.